Map of
GUMDROP'S JOURNEY
through London

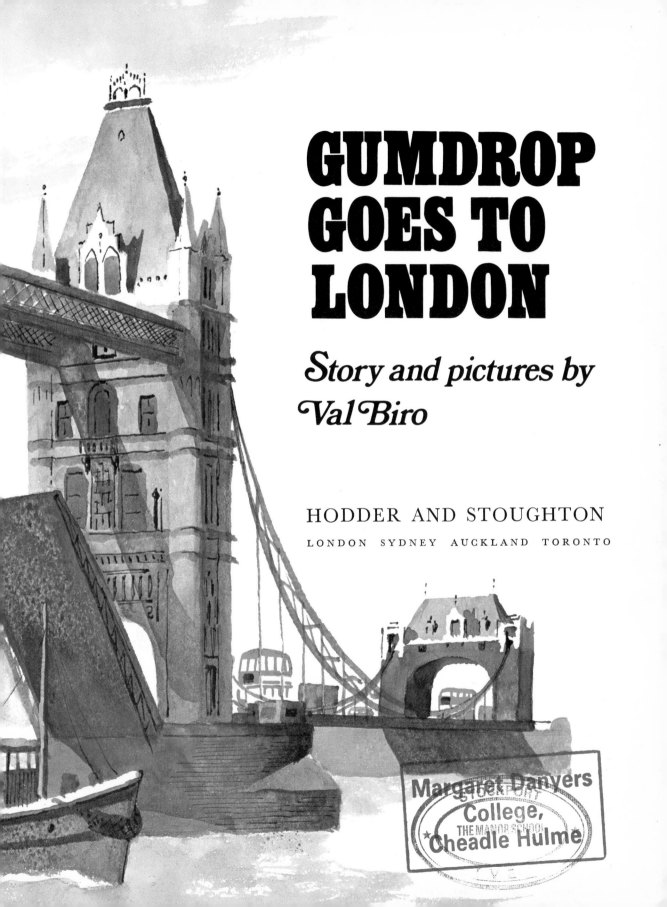

GUMDROP GOES TO LONDON

Story and pictures by
Val Biro

HODDER AND STOUGHTON
LONDON SYDNEY AUCKLAND TORONTO

MR JOSIAH OLDCASTLE lived in a small house
in the country and he liked it very much.
He had a small garden which he liked even more.
There was also a small garage with large red
doors and inside the garage was something which
Mr Oldcastle liked best of all.
It was a blue car with a black hood and a brass
horn; it had four large wheels and
four small lamps and a brass thermometer. It was
an Austin Clifton Heavy Twelve-Four, vintage 1926,
and it was called Gumdrop.

One fine morning
a letter arrived. "It is from
BBC Television in London,"
cried Mr Oldcastle, "and they want
Gumdrop to appear on a programme
tomorrow afternoon at three o'clock!"
Mr Oldcastle was delighted. "Millions of people
will see Gumdrop," he thought, "so I had better
polish him up until he shines."
And he did just that.

The sun was shining when he set out next morning, so Mr Oldcastle put Gumdrop's hood down. At a quarter to twelve they crossed Tower Bridge and drove past the Tower of London.

Suddenly a Yeoman of the Guard came hurrying towards them. "My name is Biffin, Sir, and I would be much obliged for a lift to Westminster. I can't go by bus, because they won't let this partisan of mine on board."

"Jump in, then!"
said Mr Oldcastle
and the grateful
beefeater, holding the
awkward weapon above
his head, did just that.

It was a quarter past twelve when they reached St Paul's Cathedral. Just then two men ran out of a building, jumped into a small yellow car, turned sharply into the road so that Gumdrop had to stop, and drove smartly away.

"Stop those men!" shouted a policeman who ran out of the building too and jumped into Gumdrop. "I am Sergeant Bluemantle and I was called to apprehend those persons who have just stolen five thousand pounds from the Bank. We must catch them, so please be good enough to drive as fast as you can after them!"

And Mr Oldcastle did just that.

There was heavy traffic in Fleet Street and the going was slow. The yellow car was way ahead of them. It was nearly a quarter to one by the time they reached the Law Courts, where they had to stop again.

A man in a wig was sitting in the middle of a zebra crossing, and he was very angry.
"Those uncouth villains in that impossible yellow contraption have just knocked me down! If I don't see them prosecuted for this, then my name is not Sir Pomeroy Pendlebury-Clutterbuck, Justice of Her Majesty's High Court!"
"Please get in, then," said Mr Oldcastle, and the judge did just that.

It was a quarter past one when the bandits reached Whitehall. There they suddenly turned right, drove through a gateway and disappeared.

"Follow them through the
Horseguards!" ordered Sir
Pomeroy. "And you, my men,"
calling the two mounted sentries, "follow us!"
Corporal Withers and Trooper Gaskin did just that.

It was half past one when they reached Buckingham Palace.
The bandits drove their car recklessly through the band of

the Grenadier Guards, skidded round the
Victoria Memorial and roared up
Constitution Hill.
Gumdrop was stopped by Drummer Thumpit.
"I'll make mincemeat of them for this!"
he cried and jumped in. "After them!"
And Gumdrop did just that.

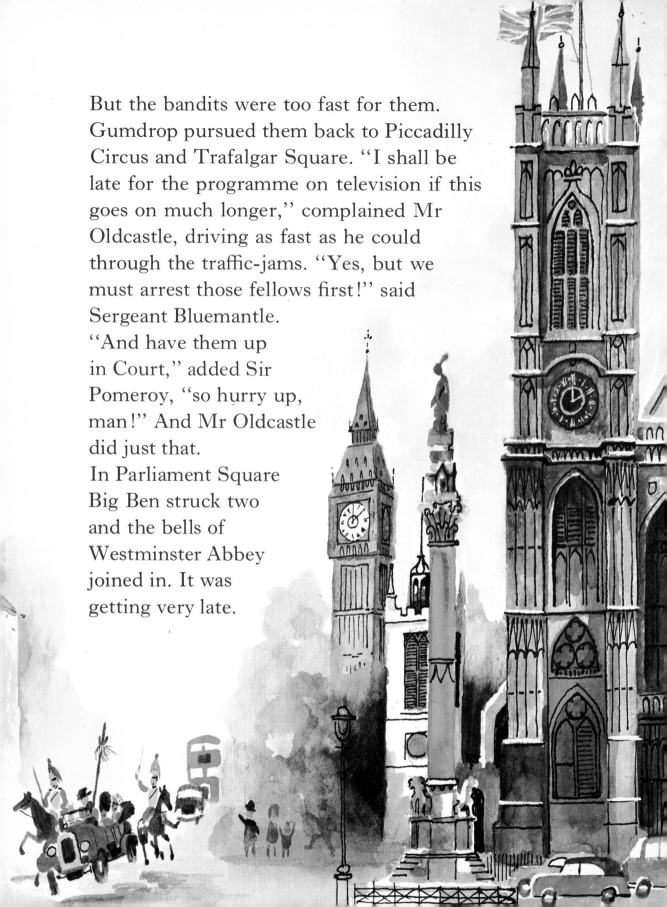

But the bandits were too fast for them. Gumdrop pursued them back to Piccadilly Circus and Trafalgar Square. "I shall be late for the programme on television if this goes on much longer," complained Mr Oldcastle, driving as fast as he could through the traffic-jams. "Yes, but we must arrest those fellows first!" said Sergeant Bluemantle. "And have them up in Court," added Sir Pomeroy, "so hurry up, man!" And Mr Oldcastle did just that.

In Parliament Square Big Ben struck two and the bells of Westminster Abbey joined in. It was getting very late.

By now the yellow car was out of sight. Gumdrop couldn't go very fast because the weight of Mr Oldcastle, Beefeater Biffin, Sergeant Bluemantle, Sir Pomeroy Pendlebury-Clutterbuck and Drummer Thumpit had slowed him down considerably. It was just as well that Corporal Withers and Trooper Gaskin had their horses to ride on.

"They went up that street there!" said Lance-Corporal Albert Gunner, a Chelsea Pensioner, when they stopped to ask him.
"Get in, then," said Mr Oldcastle, "and show us the way."
And Lance-Corporal Gunner did just that.

It was nearly half past two when they reached the Albert Hall, and it was getting extremely late. But they had to stop again to allow members of the Philharmonic Orchestra to cross over from the Albert Memorial.

"If you are chasing that yellow menace that nearly had us over just now then I will come and show you which way they went," cried Mr Owen Llewellyn the trombone player. "Indeed to goodness I will!" And he did just that.

"I shall NEVER get to Television Centre at this rate!"
protested Mr Oldcastle. He drove on as fast as he could
until they came to Shepherd's Bush.
"There they go!" cried all the passengers in Gumdrop.
"We'll catch them yet!" But the yellow car was too fast for
them again. It roared up a straight road. It was almost
out of sight when, suddenly, the bandits saw a police
car in the road. They turned their car sharply and
drove through an open gate. Gumdrop went after them and
the police car followed behind.
"Look there!" cried Mr Oldcastle in delight. "They've
brought us to where I have been trying to drive all day!"
For it was the BBC Television Centre, and it was five
minutes to three.

There was no way out for the bandits. They stopped their car, jumped out, and ran up the stairs and through the doors. Gumdrop stopped too. The passengers jumped out of Gumdrop. The policemen jumped out of the police car, and they all ran up the stairs and through the doors after the bandits.

"They might get out through the back and escape!" said Sergeant Bluemantle to Mr Oldcastle. "Let's try to head them off, then!" said Mr Oldcastle. He turned Gumdrop round and did just that.

He drove Gumdrop through a wide doorway into a curved corridor which ran round the whole building. They turned a corner and there they had to stop.

The bandits were running towards them, and all the others chasing the bandits were running too. Gumdrop was blocking the way, so the bandits opened a door and ran straight in.

It was the television studio and the time was three o'clock.

In the studio the programme had just started. Everybody else came tumbling in after the bandits. The television cameras were working as the bandits were surrounded. They were held fast by the policemen from the police car as Sergeant Bluemantle handcuffed the robbers.

So ended Gumdrop's journey to London. It had turned into a wild chase through London after two desperate bank robbers, and Mr Oldcastle had nearly missed his programme on television. But he didn't after all: instead he helped to arrest the criminals in front of the television cameras. And three million people who watched the programme saw him do it.

"This is all thanks to Gumdrop!" said the presenter of the programme to his huge audience, as Gumdrop was pushed into the studio. The cameras were still working away. "So join us now in a song to celebrate Gumdrop, that astonishing and exceptional Austin Clifton Heavy Twelve-Four, vintage 1926!"

And all the people in the studio gathered round the television camera, and all the people watching the programme gathered round their sets, and they all sang this special song for Gumdrop:

The Gumdrop Song

Oom-pa-pah, oom-pa-pah, oom-pa-oom-pa-oom-pa-pah, it's GUM-DROP —— with his

pop-pop-pop, The fin-est mo-tor car we've ev-er seen, oh

GUM-DROP, we're so glad you stopped, Every-body's looked inside,

Every-body wants a ride in old pop- pop GUM-DROP! ——

Gumdrop goes to London

ISBN 0-340-13477-1

Copyright © 1971 Val Biro
Words and music on this page copyright © Christopher Sandford

First published 1971
Sixth impression 1983

Published by Hodder and Stoughton Children's Books,
a division of Hodder and Stoughton Ltd,
Mill Road, Dunton Green, Sevenoaks, Kent TN13 2YJ

Printed in Great Britain by Springbourne Press Limited,
Basildon, Essex

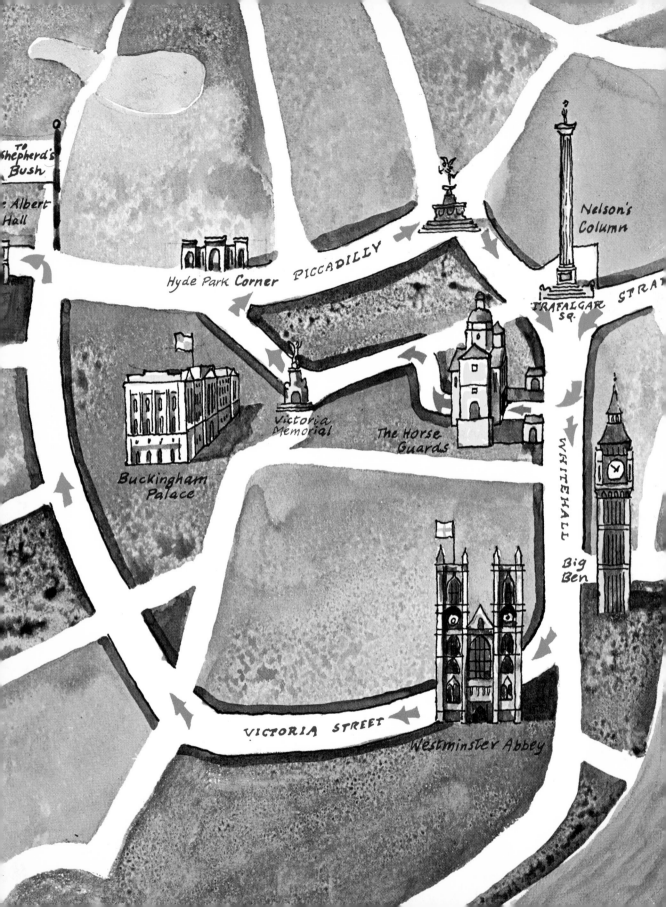